This book belongs to

_____

TWELVE LIZARDS LEAPING

A New Twelve Days of Christmas

BY Jan Romero Stevens

ILLUSTRATED BY Christine Mau

rising moon

The illustrations are acrylic on bristol board
The text type was set in Greymantle
Composed in the United States of America
Designed by Jennifer Schaber
Edited by Aimee Jackson
Production supervised by Lisa Brownfield

Printed in Hong Kong by Midas Printing Company, Ltd.

FIRST IMPRESSION
ISBN 0-87358-744-8
Library of Congress Catalog Card Number 99-17614

Stevens, Jan Romero.
Twelve lizards leaping : a new Twelve days of Christmas / written
by Jan Romero Stevens ; illustrated by Christine Mau.
p. cm.
Summary: This Southwestern version of the familiar Christmas song
features such gifts as ten tamales steaming, six piñatas swaying,
and two prickly pears.
ISBN 0–87358–744–8 (hardcover)
1. Children's songs—United States Texts. [1. Christmas music
Texts. 2. Southwest, New Songs and music. 3. Christmas music.
4. Songs.] I. Mau, Christine, 1965– ill. II. Twelve days of
Christmas (English folk song) III. Title.
PZ8.3.S843Tw 1999
782.42164'0268—dc21   99–17614

0749/7.5M/8-99

To my very wonderful husband, Fred.
—J. R. S.

To Mike, Zachary, and Sidney, with love.
—C. M.

The Twelve Days of Christmas

On the first day of Christ - mas my true love gave to me a

quail in a pa - lo - ver - de tree. On the sec-ond day of Christ - mas my

true love gave to me two prick-ly pears, and a quail in a pa - lo - ver - de

tree. On the { third fourth fifth } day of Christ - mas my true love gave to me

three horned toads, four sil-ver spurs, three horned toads,

On the first day of Christmas
my true love gave to me

a quail in a
Paloverde tree.

On the second day of Christmas
my true love gave to me

two prickly pears,

and a quail in a paloverde tree.

On the third day of Christmas
my true love gave to me

three horned toads,

two prickly pears,
and a quail in a paloverde tree.

On the fourth day of Christmas
my true love gave to me

four silver spurs,

three horned toads,

two prickly pears,

and a quail in a paloverde tree.

On the fifth day of Christmas
my true love gave to me
five turquoise rings,
four silver spurs,
three horned toads,
two prickly pears,
and a quail in a paloverde tree.

On the sixth day of Christmas
my true love gave to me

six piñatas swaying,

five turquoise rings,
four silver spurs,
three horned toads,
two prickly pears,
and a quail in a paloverde tree.

On the seventh day of Christmas
my true love gave to me

seven dancers swirling,

six piñatas swaying,

five turquoise rings,

four silver spurs,

three horned toads,

two prickly pears,

and a quail in a paloverde tree.

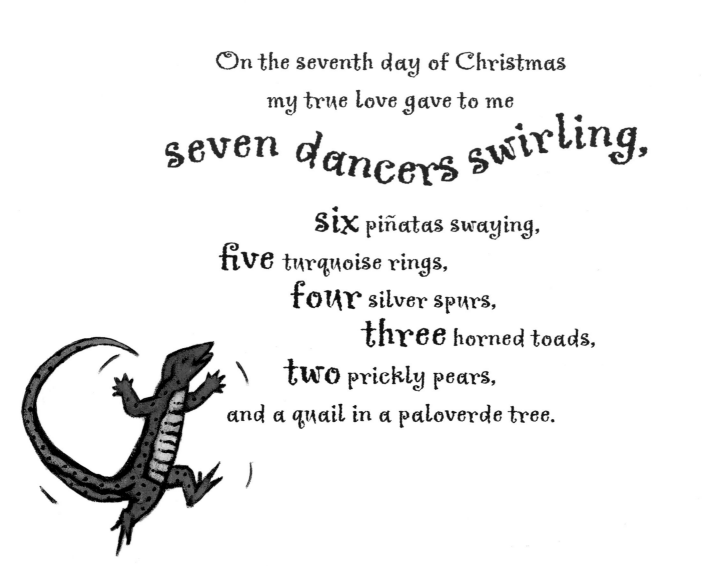

On the eighth day of Christmas
my true love gave to me

eight cowpokes twirling,

seven dancers swirling,
six piñatas swaying,
five turquoise rings,
four silver spurs,
three horned toads,
two prickly pears,
and a quail in a paloverde tree.

On the ninth day of Christmas
my true love gave to me

nine luminarias gleaming,

eight cowpokes twirling,
seven dancers swirling,
six piñatas swaying,
five turquoise rings,
four silver spurs,
three horned toads,
two prickly pears,
and a quail in a paloverde tree.

On the tenth day of Christmas
my true love gave to me
ten tamales steaming,

nine luminarias gleaming,
eight cowpokes twirling,
seven dancers swirling,
six piñatas swaying,
five turquoise rings,
four silver spurs,
three horned toads,
two prickly pears,
and a quail in a paloverde tree.

On the eleventh day of Christmas
my true love gave to me

eleven coyotes creeping,

ten tamales steaming,
nine luminarias gleaming,
eight cowpokes twirling,
seven dancers swirling,
six piñatas swaying,
five turquoise rings,
four silver spurs,
three horned toads,
two prickly pears,
and a quail in a paloverde tree.

On the twelfth day of Christmas
my true love gave to me
twelve lizards leaping,

eleven coyotes creeping,
ten tamales steaming,
nine luminarias gleaming,
eight cowpokes twirling,
seven dancers swirling,
six piñatas swaying,
five turquoise rings,
four silver spurs,
three horned toads,
two prickly pears,
and a quail in a paloverde tree.

About the Author

Jan Romero Stevens was born in Las Vegas, New Mexico, and has lived all her life in New Mexico and Arizona. Her fascination with the culture, history, food, and people of the Southwest has been the inspiration for her picture books. Jan has won devoted fans with her *Carlos* books, in which Carlos' insatiable curiosity gets him into all kinds of humorous predicaments. For instance, in *Carlos and the Squash Plant,* Carlos' refusal to take a bath results in a squash plant sprouting from his ear. Carlos' humorous antics continue to amuse readers in *Carlos and the Cornfield, Carlos and the Skunk,* and *Carlos and the Carnival,* all of which have bilingual Spanish/English texts.

Jan has been the recipient of several awards, including the 1998 Children's Author Award given by the Arizona Library Association and the 1998 Copper Quill Award from the Flagstaff Public Library. Jan lives in Flagstaff, Arizona, with her husband, Fred, and their two sons, Jacob and Paul.

About the Illustrator

Christine Mau lives on Doty Island in Neenah, Wisconsin, where she and her husband, Mike, work from home so they can enjoy raising their two sons, Zachary and Sidney. Mike is a photographer and Christine is a graphic designer and illustrator. She creates the rich texture and vivid color in her illustrations by applying acrylic paint in multiple layers with a dry brush technique, enhanced by the occasional cat hair, courtesy of her two feline assistants, Botta and Makeda.

Christine specializes in design and illustration development of product and packaging graphics for Kimberly-Clark Corporation, and has illustrated for several children's publications. She has been the recipient of many Addy awards for design at both the district and national levels and her artwork has been exhibited at many galleries throughout Wisconsin. This is Christine's first picture book.